UNITED STATES

WORLD ADVENTURES

BY STEFFI CAVELL-CLARKE

KidHaven
PUBLISHING

Published in 2019 by
KidHaven Publishing, an Imprint of Greenhaven Publishing, LLC
353 3rd Avenue, Suite 255, New York, NY 10010

© 2019 Booklife Publishing

This edition is published by arrangement with Booklife Publishing.

Designer: Natalie Carr
Editor: Grace Jones
Writer: Steffi Cavell-Clarke

Cataloging-in-Publication Data

Names: Cavell-Clarke, Steffi.
Title: United States / Steffi Cavell-Clarke.
Description: New York : KidHaven Publishing, 2019. | Series: World adventures | Includes index.
Identifiers: ISBN 9781534526044 (pbk.) | 9781534526037 (library bound) | ISBN 9781534526051 (6 pack) | ISBN 9781534526068 (ebook)
Subjects: LCSH: United States–Juvenile literature.
Classification: LCC E178.3 C38 2019 | DDC 973–dc23

Printed in the United States of America

CPSIA compliance information: Batch # BS18KL: For further information contact Greenhaven Publishing LLC, New York, New York at 1-844-317-7404.

CONTENTS

Words in **red** can be found in the glossary on page 24.

WHERE IS THE UNITED STATES OF AMERICA?

The United States of America is a country found in North America. It is made up of 50 areas called states.

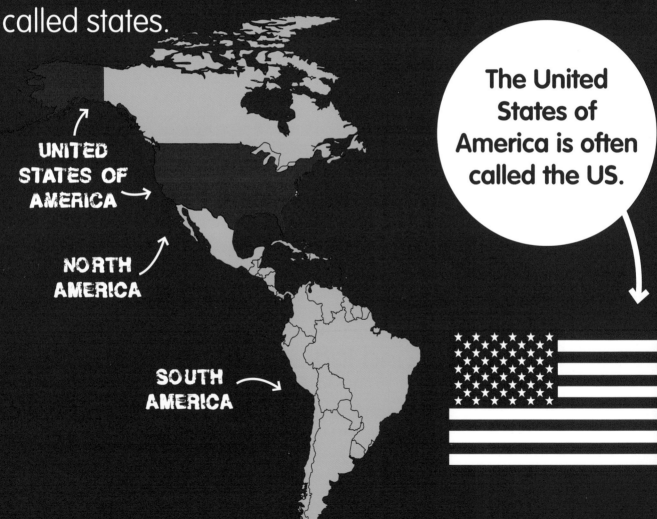

UNITED STATES OF AMERICA →

NORTH AMERICA

SOUTH AMERICA →

The United States of America is often called the US.

The **population** of the US is over 325 million people. Many people in the US live in large cities, such as New York City and Los Angeles.

WASHINGTON, D.C.

The capital city of the US

WEATHER AND LANDSCAPE

The weather in the US changes across the country. Some parts of the US have extreme weather, such as tornadoes.

TORNADO

There are many different types of landscapes in the US. There are mountains, forests, and rivers.

The Missouri River is the longest river in the US.

MISSOURI RIVER

CLOTHING

In the US, athletic shoes are called sneakers.

Many people living in the US dress in cool and comfortable clothing, such as jeans and T-shirts.

Blue jeans are very popular in the US. They are made from a **material** called denim.

JEANS

RELIGION

The **religion** with the most followers in the US is Christianity. Christians celebrate special events throughout the year, such as Christmas.

There are also people in the US who follow other religions, such as Judaism, Islam, and Hinduism.

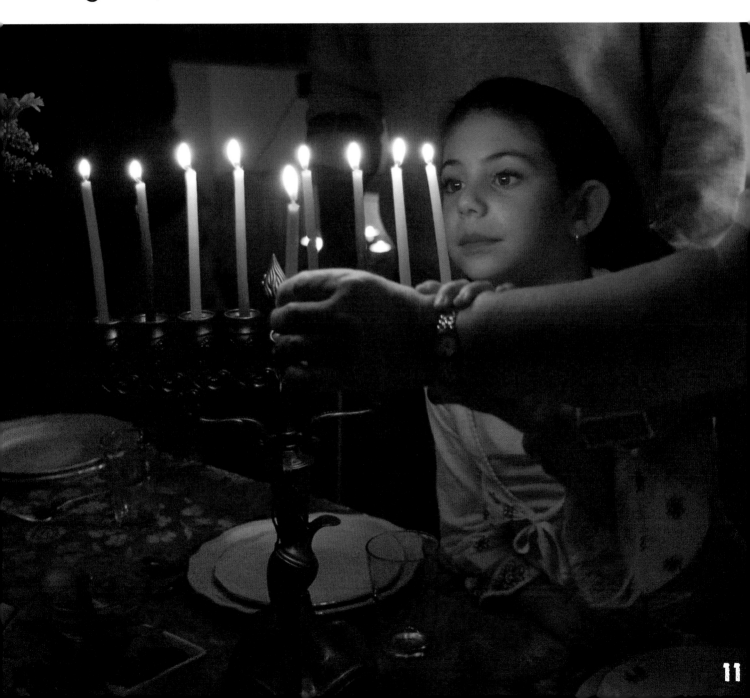

FOOD

DESSERT

Apple pie is a popular dish in the US. It is made from baked apples and pastry.

Hot dogs are also very popular in the US. A hot dog is a cooked sausage in a sliced bun.

HOT DOG

AT SCHOOL

Children starting school in the US go to **kindergarten** in their first year. In kindergarten, children learn how to draw, read, and write.

After the first year in kindergarten, children move through school grades each year, from first grade to twelfth grade.

AT HOME

Apartments in New York City

Many people in the US live in large cities. In most cities, there are people who live in apartments in tall buildings.

In towns and villages, many people live in houses. Many houses built in the US have porch areas. People often use these to sit on.

PORCH

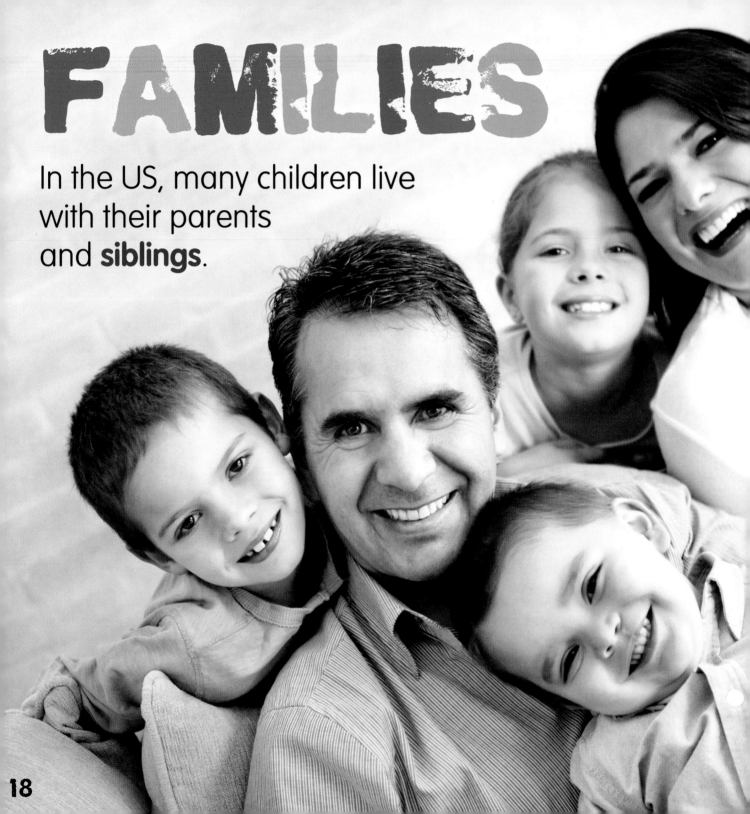

FAMILIES

In the US, many children live with their parents and **siblings**.

Many families in the US like to get together to celebrate special occasions, such as **Thanksgiving**.

SPORTS

FOOTBALL

People in the US are known for enjoying many different types of sports. One of the most popular sports is football.

Every year a huge football game called the Super Bowl takes place. Thousands of people go to watch.

THE SUPER BOWL

FUN FACTS

Neil Armstrong was an astronaut from the US. He was the first person to walk on the moon.

He said "That's one small step for a man, one giant leap for mankind."

NEIL ARMSTRONG

There are many farms and ranches in the US. On ranches, people take care of animals like horses and cows.

GLOSSARY

astronaut someone who is trained to go up into space

extreme dangerous and serious

kindergarten the first year of formal school in the US

material fabric or cloth

population number of people living in a place

religion the belief in and worship of a god or gods

siblings brothers and sisters

Thanksgiving a national holiday in the United States of America

tornadoes fast-moving, strong winds that form into funnel shapes

INDEX